EASTER

 HiGH CONTRAST **+**  **CLEAR SHAPES** **=**

Chick

Bunny

Lamb

Bee

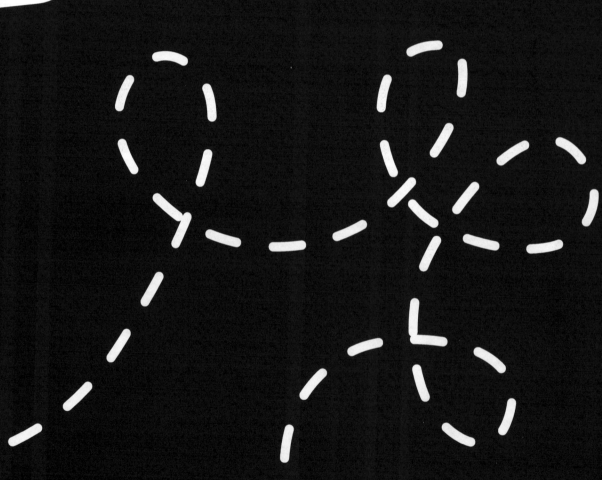

Bunny Painting Easter Eggs

Easter Eggs

Bouquet
of
Flowers

Happy Chick

Watering Can

Rooster

Carrots

Ladybug
&
Mushroom

Chocolate Bunny.

Cupcake

Chick

Duck

Duck
&
Easter Eggs

Easter Basket

illustrations:
Freepik
Vecteezy

if that's not a problem for you,
i would be very gratefu
l if you could leave
your review on my Amazon page.
Every opinion means the world
to me because it helps
me improve my products so that they will
be made to perfection just for you!

SIMON HARRIS
publishing

Made in the USA
Monee, IL
02 April 2024

56182665R00022